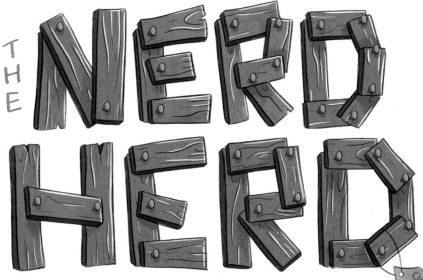

THE NERD HERD

Book 3

For the nieces & nephews: Kaitlin, Emily, Jess, Hannah, Dominic, Lylah, Mackenzie & Cruz–NL

For Bruce and Fran, thanks for welcoming me into your herd all those years ago! xxx–CK

Scholastic Australia
An imprint of Scholastic Australia Pty Limited
PO Box 579 Gosford NSW 2250
ABN 11 000 614 577
www.scholastic.com.au

Part of the Scholastic Group
Sydney • Auckland • New York • Toronto • London • Mexico City • New Delhi • Hong Kong • Buenos Aires • Puerto Rico

Published by Scholastic Australia in 2021.
Text copyright © Nathan Luff, 2021.
Illustrations copyright © Chris Kennett, 2021.
Cover design by Hannah Janzen.
Internal design by Elly Whiley.

The moral rights of Nathan Luff have been asserted.
The moral rights of Chris Kennett have been asserted.

 A catalogue record for this book is available from the
NATIONAL LIBRARY OF AUSTRALIA
National Library of Australia

ISBN: 978-1-76097-462-6

Typeset in Apertura, Blorp, Knicknack, Agent 'C' and Pequena Pro.
Printed in China by Hang Tai Printing Company Limited.
Scholastic Australia's policy, in association with Hang Tai, is to use papers that are renewable and made efficiently from wood grown in responsibly managed forests, so as to minimise its environmental footprint.

10 9 8 7 6 5 4 3 2 1   21 22 23 24 25 / 2

THE NERD HERD

OUTFOXED

Book 3

NATHAN LUFF

CHRIS KENNETT

A Scholastic Australia book

PREVIOUSLY . . .

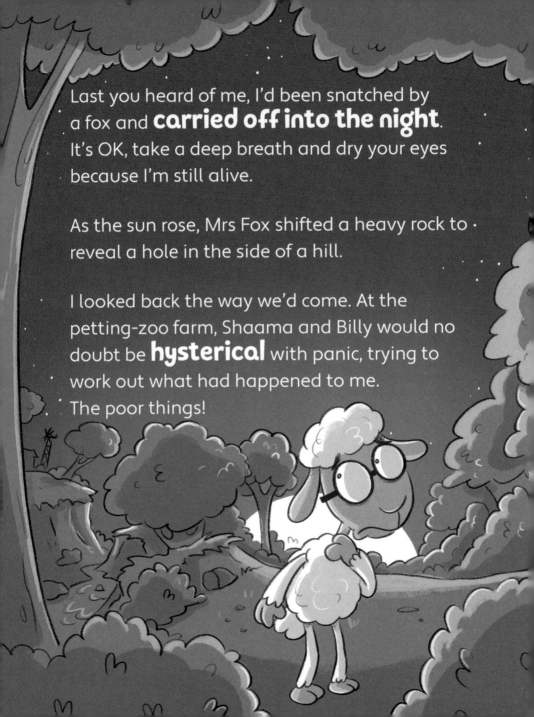

Last you heard of me, I'd been snatched by a fox and **carried off into the night**. It's OK, take a deep breath and dry your eyes because I'm still alive.

As the sun rose, Mrs Fox shifted a heavy rock to reveal a hole in the side of a hill.

I looked back the way we'd come. At the petting-zoo farm, Shaama and Billy would no doubt be **hysterical** with panic, trying to work out what had happened to me. The poor things!

CHAPTER ONE

A NEW NARRATOR

Barny has asked me to tell you about what happened that morning since he wasn't there.

So, let's see . . .

We woke up, outside (yet again). It's fine for the others but I really feel the cold. Also, my magnificent mohair is not waterproof. Angora goats are better suited to the indoors. We deserve **pampering**.

What was I talking about again?
Oh yeah, what happened, so . . .

We ate some grass.

We took in the beautiful scenery.

I did some yoga.

'FLOATING GOAT'

'CRACKIN BACK'

'BUM TWISTER'

'SMELL THE CHEESE'

'ANGRY PRETZEL'

It was a pretty normal morning except Barny was very quiet. I didn't care because I wasn't talking to him—he was responsible for my leech attack, and both my first and second **electrocutions**.

Barny was also being very still. Overall, he was acting **sheepish**, which should make sense because he is a sheep, but Barny never acts like he should.

He's annoying like that.

Around midday I asked Shaama 'How long do you think Barny is going to be like this? It's unnerving.'

'Like what?'

I pointed to Barny. 'Like that.'

'Like a **pile of hay?**' she said.
'Yes, exactly! That's a good way of putting it.'
'Billy, that's not Barny. That *is* a pile of hay,'
Shaama said.
I blew my fringe clear and had a better look.

Shaama was right.

So where was Barny?

Shaama wanted to go look for him. I was in favour of adding facial features to the pile of hay and calling it Barny. **Barny-the-hay-pile** would get us into a lot less trouble and we wouldn't have to suffer through any more **terrible jokes**.

Shaama agreed to do the searching because, as she pointed out, I couldn't tell the difference between our friend and our breakfast. Harsh but true.

I remained under our tree and snuck in a **beauty nap**. I have this recurring dream where I'm a runway model . . .

Shaama shook me awake.

Barny's not anywhere and he wouldn't just disappear like that. Something's wrong.

SHAKE

SHAKE

'Did you check under **Kevin Bacon?**' I asked, yawning. When that pig decides to sit on you, you could be stuck there for hours. Trust me!

Shaama nodded. 'He wasn't th—' she stopped speaking suddenly and gasped. 'What's that?' She pointed to my fleece. I looked down to see a clump of coarse **hair**. I shrieked. All the stress was turning my fleece **feral!**

'Calm down, it's not attached.' Shaama picked the hair off. 'But I recognise this hair. This belongs to **Mrs Fox!**'

Shaama stashes gross second-hand things in a tree trunk—things she believes might be useful one day. She dug around and found a map.

'This is our petting-zoo farm here.' She pointed out a section. 'These are our neighbours and at the end of our street is a nature reserve. I bet Mrs Fox's **den** is there, with Barny inside.'

NATURE RESERVE

NEIGHBOUR'S PROPERTY

NATURE RESERVE

'No, **absolutely** not!' I said, knowing exactly what Shaama was proposing we do.

'Billy, if anything happened to you, Barny would come running, no questions asked,' Shaama said.

That was only because Barny was an **idiot**.

'Does your map show the fences and gates and people stopping us from getting out to the street in the first place?' I asked.

'Hmmm, I guess we need a **plan**,' Shaama said.

Barny usually comes up with the plans. They're always bad. But a bad plan is better than no plan. I try to come up with plans but my brain doesn't work the same way.

This is how my brain works:

'So, any ideas?' Shaama asked. I stopped swishing and shook my head instead.

'Look, some **sheepies!**' a man cried out. He was heading our way, struggling with an enormous pram.

Sheepies? I look nothing like a common sheep. 'I can't believe you're asleep,' the man said, looking inside the pram. 'You're missing everything.' He pulled the hood of the pram down to protect his child from the sun. Shaama was smiling.

Oh Billy, I have a very Barny-esque idea!

23

CHAPTER TWO

A DINNER INVITATION

It's **Barny** here again.

So, while Billy and Shaama were desperately searching for their best friend in the whole entire world, Mrs Fox was trying to get me to enter her den. I had a plan though. I was going to push her inside and roll the rock back over to seal her in.

As Mrs Fox **bulldozed** me forward with her head, pushing me deep underground, I wondered if I should have acted a little more quickly.

'I've brought company,' Mrs Fox called out.
Oh great, Mrs Fox didn't live alone.
I'm a lamb—I'm not equipped for situations like these.

An **abridged** list of defence mechanisms in the animal kingdom :

A complete list of a lamb's defence mechanisms:

Soon I would be surrounded by foxes, maybe even hungry little baby foxes. I may as well have walked around with a sign that read: **ALL YOU CAN EAT BUFFET**.

The darkened tunnel opened into a room that was eerily lit by jars of glowworms.
'**Nice digs**,' I said, with a wink.
Billy and Shaama would have appreciated the joke.

Digs? Get it—because it's a burrow . . . because you dug it . . .

A large rustic table took up most of the space and sitting on top of it was an **enormous cake**. I leaned forward to inspect the cake and a rotten smell hit me like a brick. The black and white icing was oozing all over the place. Actually, it wasn't icing. It was a layer of **crawling ants, flies and maggots**.

I took a large step back.

There were entrances to other tunnels and from one of them came the four old chooks Mrs Fox had previously stolen from the petting-zoo farm:

Janine

Jill

Lorraine

Elaine

I was shocked to see them alive.

'Hang on a second!' I said. 'What's happening here?'

Mrs Fox pulled out a seat for me. 'It's a **dinner party**, of course! I simply adore entertaining.' Mrs Fox roughly guided me into my seat while the chooks found their own.

'When my husband **deserted** me on our wedding night,' Mrs Fox explained, 'I went from being bright eyed and bushy tailed to being a misery guts. I sat here for weeks, alone, staring at our wedding cake.'

You don't think it's time to get rid of it?' I asked, holding my nose.

'I know I should but I still have hope the smell will entice him back,' she said miserably.

I wondered if the smell was what caused him to leave in the first place.

'You can't imagine how lonely I was,' Mrs Fox continued, 'and hungry I might add. Fortunately, I was struck by a **cunning** plan. I decided to invite my prey to dinner; to enjoy them first as company, and then as my meal. It's a **two for one deal!**'

My eyes shot open in alarm. Was I about to be **eaten?**

Surely you don't eat *all* your dinner guests! The chooks are still alive.

'Yes but that's only because I love **party games** before dinner and it's much more fun with extra players. I decided to keep this lot as permanent guests. To be fair, old chicken tastes a bit stringy anyway.'

SHRUG

Rude! Oh and she means 'keep' literally. We're prisoners, not guests.

I stood up.
'Look, I'm honoured to be invited over but I have to get back to my friends. They'll be so worried about where I am. I mean the world to them—'

Mrs Fox smiled slyly. 'Oh no, dinner guests **never leave!**'

CHAPTER THREE

EYES WIDE OPEN

You're back at the petting-zoo farm with me, beautiful Billy.

Remember the man Shaama and I saw earlier with the pram? Well, he really struggled to push that pram out through the exit gate.

44

'Someone must have a **heavy nappy**,' he said. 'An *extremely* heavy nappy.'

He wheeled the pram to his car and pulled the hood off to access his child.
He got quite a surprise.

'What are these dirty old **stuffed toys** doing in here?' the man asked.

Dirty?
Old?
Stuffed?

It's one thing to have a grotty child's hands all over you but it's quite another to be insulted like that.

Excuse me, I'm beautiful!

The man's screams were higher-pitched than mine usually are. That's impressive!

Shaama and I wrestled out of the toddler's grip and the pram toppled, throwing us free.

The man caught his child with one arm and used the other to shoo us away.

Shaama spat and boy, could that child cry. Word of warning: don't ever call Shaama a giraffe-sheep, or an alpaca for that matter. Llamas are very **sensitive** like that.

So, we'd made it outside the farm gates. Shaama consulted the map and dashed away with me running to catch up. At the end of the street, like she'd said, there was a nature reserve.

PUFF

PANT

A dirt path led steeply down into a gully. I'd been enjoying the concrete we'd been walking on. It had been flat, smooth and very clean. By comparison the dirt looked very . . . **dirty**.

Shaama **pushed** me.

I stumbled down the incline, barely keeping my balance as I brushed up against branches and bushes. It was impossible to stop or to slow down. The ragged path set my fringe bouncing and I could only see things in flashes.

The flash of a tree in the distance.

The flash of a tree much closer.

The flash of a tree trunk right up close.

The flash of pain.

THONK!

Then darkness.

'I hate you, **Shaama Llama Ding Dong**,'
I said upon regaining consciousness. My head
was throbbing. My beautiful coat was a mess
after I'd snagged all sorts of seeds and burrs.

Shaama produced a couple of hair scrunchies.
'Oh, I forgot. I brought these from my tree trunk
to keep your fringe out of your eyes.'

Hold still!

Shaama launched a surprise makeover on me
while I screamed and struggled.

'You are *not* a trained professional!' I kept shouting.

Once done, Shaama stood back to appraise my new hairstyle.

'**Foxy?** Like a fox?' I asked.
'No, *foxy* is an expression. It means you look really attractive.'
I wasn't entirely surprised. Most things look good on me.

'Well, let's get this over with,' I said, holding my head proud. 'What am I looking for?'

'We need to find the entrance to Mrs Fox's den,' Shaama said. 'We also still need a plan as to what we're going to do if we find it.'

A plan.
We needed a plan.

We'd have to deal
with the nasty fox.

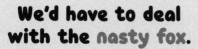

That's ridiculous calling
someone foxy when
they're attractive.

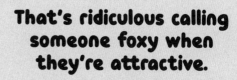

Why don't they say,
'Wow, you're looking
goaty?' That makes
way more sense.

I'm looking really
goaty today.

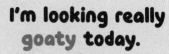

Especially with
my new hair-do.
I'm goaty to
the extreme.

'Any ideas?' Shaama asked.
'Ahh, not yet,' I said.

Turns out the nature reserve we were in was full of holes. Big holes, medium holes, small holes. The task was impossible. I was prepared to give up after the first hole but Shaama dragged me onwards.

With my fringe up, it was like I was seeing the world properly for the first time. The bugs ... the grime ... the pollen ... **the spider webs!**

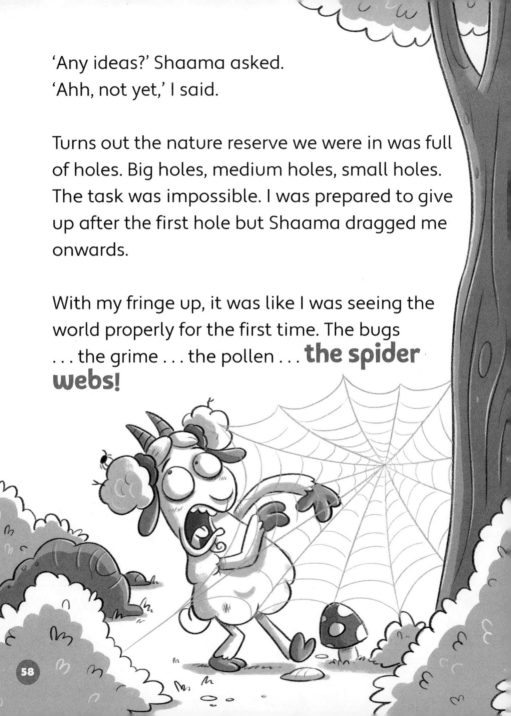

Eventually Shaama found a hole that made her smile.

'Fox hair everywhere,' she said. '**We've found it!**'

I looked at the hole leading into darkness.

'I think it's important one of us stays outside to keep guard,' I said, quickly sitting myself down.

CHAPTER FOUR

PARTY GAMES

Mrs Fox clapped her paws together. 'Ladies, should we have some music?'

I could do a show tune. Something from *Harespray* or *Jersey Cows*?

I prefer hip hop like in that *Ham-ilton* show.

That isn't music. That's just noise.

Speak for yourself. I lay eggs *and* sick beats.

You're embarrassing yourself.

'Enough!' Mrs Fox shouted and the chooks stopped squabbling. 'What party game should we begin with then? Charades? Ohhh, guess this story title. Two words.'
Mrs Fox pointed to Jill.

I love charades! I couldn't help but lean forward and shout out answers.

Jill? Hen? Old? Feathers? Chook? Chicken?

'**Yes, chicken!**' Mrs Fox cried. 'Now the second word.'

Mrs Fox stuck out her long tongue and licked Jill.

Ummm . . . **Chicken** food?
Chicken dinner?
Chicken stock?

'No, no, look at what I'm doing.' Mrs Fox kept licking Jill, up and down.

LICK

LICK

LICK

'Chicken... **tongue?** Chicken... **kiss?** Chicken... **flavour?** I don't know, **do something different**.'

Mrs Fox became frustrated and stomped her foot. 'It's very obviously *Chicken Licken*. I was lick-en the chicken!'

'Ohhh, of course,' I said. It was obvious once she'd said it.

Mrs Fox sighed. 'I wish Mr Fox was here—he's a **games wizard**. He would have guessed it in a heartbeat. How about some party tricks instead? Who likes magic?'

The chooks all clucked with delight.

I will read your mind— think of a number between six and eight.

She only waited a second.

The number is
seven!

She's amazing!

How did she do it?

Wait a minute—

Mrs Fox ignored me and instead she fetched a black hat from inside one of the tunnels. The hat was moving and I could hear a muffled voice calling out for help.

'This hat is empty,' Mrs Fox declared.

'Are you sure about that?' I asked.

'Now, I wave my hand like so and **presto!**' Mrs Fox pulled out a **terrified rabbit** from the hat.

Mrs Fox shoved it back inside the hat.

'Is this some sort of joke?' I asked, which was a mistake. Mrs Fox advanced towards me.

I know another trick—I could make you **disappear**,' she said, licking her lips. 'Wait, no, you can't!' I had to think of a way to **outfox** the fox. 'What I meant was . . . is it some sort of joke that we're having a dinner party and we don't even have **party costumes?**'

I clenched, waiting to be bitten.

Mrs Fox narrowed her eyes. She circled me like I was prey.

Suddenly, her ears pricked up. 'Oh, I've got it! I've got it! I'll be back in a second.' She snapped up Janine in her mouth and disappeared down a tunnel.

What is happening?

It took me a few seconds to fully appreciate that Mrs Fox had left me unsupervised.

I needed to run.

I needed to bust out of there.

I needed to seize the moment like the **brave young lamb** that I was.

Lorraine pecked me on the head.

The peck stirred me into action.

'Escape with me,' I cried.

The rabbit jumped out of the hat and attached himself to my leg. The chooks, however, looked uncertain.

I looked around at all the tunnels but couldn't remember which tunnel we'd come down. 'At least tell me which tunnel leads out?' The chooks ignored me. There was no time to waste. I chose a tunnel at random and just hoped it was the right one.

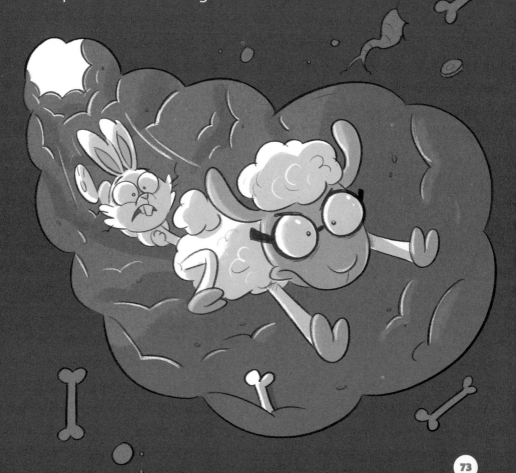

CHAPTER FIVE

THE WRONG TUNNEL

It was not the right tunnel.

It led to a room littered with **bones**—probably
the remains of previous party guests.
'She's a **monster**,' the rabbit cried.
I turned to get out of there and tripped,
knocking over a pile of bones. A ribcage came
crashing down, landing on top of both the
rabbit and one of my legs. Other bones fell on
top of the ribcage, holding it securely in place.

I tried removing my hoof but it was stuck. I tried
shifting the bones off us but they held strong.
We were **trapped**.

'This is actually quite a **humerus** situation,' I said. I waited for the rabbit to laugh but he didn't.

Humerus? Get it? It's a type of bone. Humerus as in humorous. No? Nothing?

You're a monster.

Within a mound of newly exposed bones,
I noticed **two eyes** staring out at us.

Hey, you over there,
can you give us a hand?

There was a brief pause and then the hand bones of some animal came flying over, landing near us.

CLACKITY

CLACK

It wasn't exactly what I had in mind. '**Shhhhh**,' the owner of the eyes said. 'She'll find me!'

The rabbit hopped furiously up and down while I pushed and pulled at the ribcage holding us in place. Little by little, I could feel the bones shifting but it was taking forever.

Mrs Fox's voice sang out. 'Oh, little lamb, I've got a surprise for you!'

The ribcage tumbled free but it was too late— our opportunity to escape had passed. Struck by an idea, I dragged the ribcage behind me as the rabbit and I crept through the tunnel and back into the dining room.

Janine appeared first and it certainly was a surprise. A minute ago she had been fully feathered but now she was completely **naked**.

Avert your eyes!

Oh no, she's planning on eating us after all.

I can't look!

Mrs Fox sprang into the room with a feather boa draped over her shoulders.
That explained why Janine was naked.
'How about this for a **party costume?**' Mrs Fox asked.

It's good, isn't it?
Do you want one?
I could make you one.

The other chooks looked very nervous.

'Ladies,' I whispered. 'Don't you want to be free-range again?'

'I don't know. The conditions aren't that bad,' Elaine said.

'You say that because **YOU'RE NOT NAKED!**' Janine squawked. 'I'm with the lamb. This has gone too far!'

Mrs Fox approached. 'Another party game? We could have a **dance battle?** I'm particularly good at the **foxtrot**.'

'Which tunnel leads outside?' I whispered. Janine bobbed her head towards one of the tunnels.

It was now or never.

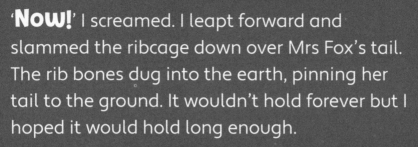

'**NOW!**' I screamed. I leapt forward and slammed the ribcage down over Mrs Fox's tail. The rib bones dug into the earth, pinning her tail to the ground. It wouldn't hold forever but I hoped it would hold long enough.

I raced down the tunnel with the chooks following close behind. Halfway through, however, the path was blocked by something both soft and hard. Something bony and yet woolly.

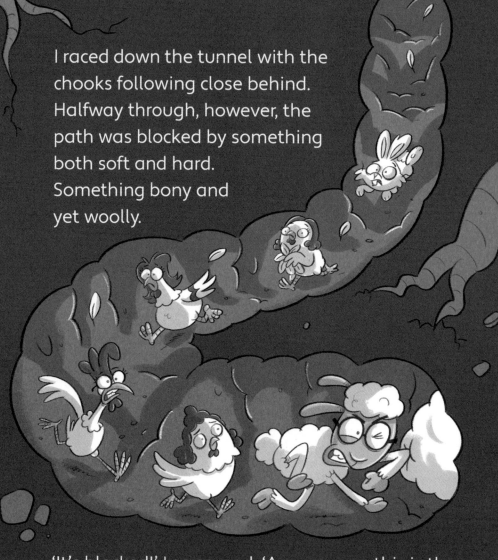

'It's blocked!' I screamed. 'Are you sure this is the right tunnel?'
I **rammed** it again with no success.

'Do you mind?' Shaama said.
It was **Shaama Llama Ding Dong!**
She'd come to **save me**. I was so happy I
could have kissed her. In fact I did kiss her.

Do that again
and I'll spit.

'Shaama, I'm so happy to see you!'
'Billy's waiting outside.'
'Amazing, let's go.' I tried pushing forward.
Shaama remained still. 'Quick, Shaama, Mrs
Fox is hot on our tails!' Still she wouldn't move.
'So, interesting fact,' she eventually said.
'Llamas are bigger than most people expect.
Also, in related news, I'm **stuck**.'

'I knew we should have stayed put,' Elaine said. 'But, no, we had to listen to old **nudey rudey** over here. She'll eat us for sure now!' I felt hot breath on my neck and when I turned around I could make out a huge grin on Mrs Fox's face.

'Well, well, well, it looks like we have some **alpaca** to add to the menu,' Mrs Fox said. Shaama spat.

PATOO!

CHAPTER SIX

PREPARING A BUFFET

Mrs Fox squeezed past, crushing me against the wall. She took Shaama's neck in her mouth and pulled. Little by little, bit by bit, Shaama shifted.

This is humiliating.

The chooks and I had no choice but to scamper out of the way and wait by the dining table, as far away from the stench of the cake as possible. We gathered in a huddle.

'We have to stick together,' I said. 'You guys are now honorary members of **The Nerd Herd**, OK? We're a team!'

Janine poked me. 'Who made you boss? Ohh, you're soft! I'm going to ask Mrs Fox to shear you before she eats you so I can knit myself a cardigan.'

'I wouldn't mind some booties while you're at it,' Elaine said.

So much for 'team'.

Mrs Fox tumbled into the cavern, followed by Shaama.

Mrs Fox stood up, blocking the exit tunnel. She turned to face us. '**Disappointing**. Now I'll have to eat you out of principle.'

Mrs Fox took a step forward, a glint in her eye.

Barny, we need one of your ridiculous plans.

No problem. **Ridiculous plans** are what I do best.

I hid myself behind Shaama. 'Look at me, Mrs Fox!' I shouted, popping up and then hiding again. I repeated this and each time, I counted aloud.

'What on earth are you doing?' Shaama asked.

'When people count sheep they **fall asleep**,' I explained. 'Is it working? Does she look sleepy?' Shaama grabbed me. 'Barny, I didn't mean a plan *that* ridiculous!'

OK, Plan B then.
'Mrs, Fox, how about we play **hide-and-seek?**' I asked, thinking we could escape while she was counting.
Mrs Fox lunged and I only just managed to dive out of the way.

Why would you suggest that game? I HATE that game!

I'd landed near the bone room's entrance, which gave me a new idea. I grabbed Shaama and dragged her inside.

'I'll distract her while you make us some type of weapon out of these,' I said.

Shaama looked puzzled.

I returned to distract Mrs Fox.
'Fine, no hide-and-seek. Let's have that dance battle you mentioned,' I shouted.
Mrs Fox's anger turned to sadness.

Mr Fox always won our dance battles. He was insanely competitive.

'So am I!' I said, taking to the dance floor.

Janine provided the beats while the other three chooks took their seats as judges. I've received many compliments for my dancing—mostly from myself—but I must admit, Mrs Fox was a strong competitor.

THE EGGS FACTOR

We danced both classic and contemporary moves. I even invented a new move I call **The Electric Fence**.

Afterwards, Mrs Fox addressed the judges.
'Be *very* careful who you pick,' she said, plucking
a feather from Jill's back.
'Mrs Fox wins!' Jill squawked.
I was **robbed**.

Shaama exited the bone room holding the weapon she'd made.

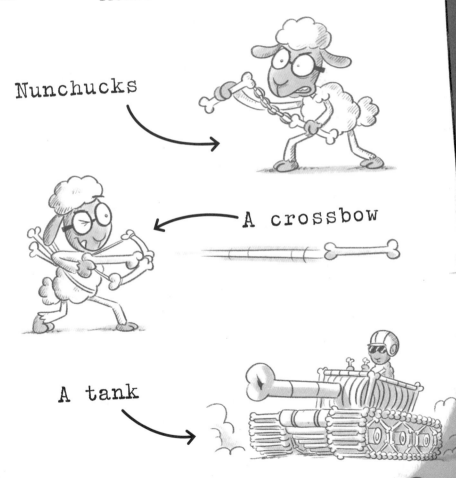

Amazing Weapons You Could Make From Bones

Nunchucks

A crossbow

A tank

Shaama was carrying a single bone.
That's it.
It was a little underwhelming.

I snatched the bone off Shaama and turned to face Mrs Fox.
'Mrs Fox, how about a game of **piñata?**'
'Yay,' she squealed.

'Good, you get to be the piñata!' Before I could attack, Mrs Fox rushed forward and tied the feather boa tightly around my head.

'The rules are that you're **blindfolded**,' she explained. She also turned me around three times to disorient me. I tried ripping the blindfold off but it was on too tight.

'Come get me,' she called.

I would have to attack Mrs Fox based on sound alone.

I lunged and missed . . .

Feathers flew everywhere.

CHAPTER SEVEN

BILLY, DON'T BE A HERO

It's me again, beautiful Billy.

Shaama had been gone for quite some time. It didn't feel right. Something must have gone wrong. I lay down for a beauty nap to rest my nerves.

When I awoke, there was still no sign of Shaama, or Barny, or the fox. I peered down the dirty, narrow entrance.

There was a song playing in my head. A song the farmer's wife often plays.

♪ ♩ ♫ ♩

Billy, don't be a hero . . .

♩ ♫ ♩

If I waited too long, it might be too late. *I could fetch help*, I thought. But who? **Ringo** wouldn't help. **Plus-Sized Puss** and **Kevin Bacon** wouldn't help. **Barny-the-hay-pile** certainly wouldn't help.
There was no-one left.
No-one but me.

♫ ♩ ♩ ♩

Billy, don't be a hero . . .

♪ ♩ ♫

Even if I wanted to be a hero, I couldn't. What skills did I have? I wasn't a hero. The only thing I was good at was cheerleading.

Billy, you gorgeous creature, listen to me—you can do this! Who got the gate shut and locked T-Bone the bull away? It was you.

I can't do it. I'm too soft.

Yes, you're soft—so soft, so beautiful, so
beautifully soft—you're divine . . .
but you're also more than that!
You're determined. You're strong.
And you're the most important
member of The Nerd Herd!

I am!

Your friends need you.

My friends need me!

Billy, *be* a hero!

I charged. I didn't think about the dirt brushing up against my fleece. I didn't think about what was going to be at the end of the tunnel. I didn't think.

The tunnel grew lighter and then Mrs Fox was there, so I lowered my head and I **rammed** her.

My poor horns. First the tree and now this. My horns are purely **decorative!**

I better not have chipped a horn!

The impact knocked Mrs Fox against the wall, where she crumbled.

I did it! I beat the fox! I was a **hero!**

'Owww,' Mrs Fox moaned before passing out.

Seconds later, Barny jumped out into the open with feathers covering his face.
'Found you, piñata, now take this!' Barny **whacked** me hard with a bone.

Then he whacked me again, and again. I fell backwards and landed on the edge of a table, flipping it. An enormous cake shot into the air and as it sailed by, I caught the whiff of decay. I saw the maggots crawling over it.

Then the cake landed.
On.
Me.

AAAAAHHH!

'Billy, you're here!' Shaama cried, once I'd fallen into a silent, zombie state.

Shaama ripped the blindfold off Barny and when he caught sight of me, he recoiled in disgust.

I rose unsteadily. I could feel things crawling through my mohair and the rotten smell was overpowering. 'You, Barny, *you* happened to me!' I staggered away from what was left of the cake but the smell travelled with me.

PONG!

The smell *was* me.

'What about your hairdo?' Barny asked.
'I didn't do that.'
I saw my reflection in Barny's large glasses.
I looked **RIDICULOUS!**

'Shaama,' I said, shaking with rage. 'You said I looked foxy.'

You've goat to be kidding, right? Get it? *Goat* to be *kid*ding. Goat. Kid. No? Because you're a goat *and* a kid.

'We really should have stuck with **Barny-the-hay-pile**,' Shaama said.

Mrs Fox started stirring.
'Quick, let's get out of here. I'll need a push.'

Shaama wanted a push? She deserved one, that's for sure. They both did. Screaming, I **rammed** Shaama as hard as I could and I kept ramming her all the way through the tunnel until we came out the other end. Some chooks and a rabbit followed us out. I ignored them and rammed Shaama again.

Stop! Stop! Stop! Where's Barny?

CHAPTER EIGHT

HOME ON THE RANGE

I was about to follow Billy and Shaama when I heard Mrs Fox sobbing.

I know I should have left while I had the chance. I know that she wanted to eat me. I guess I'm not only soft on the outside.

But then I was struck by a sudden thought.
'Wait a minute, Mrs Fox. Did you say Mr Fox was extremely **competitive** at games?'
She nodded.
'And on the night he left, were you playing **hide-and-seek?**'
Her ears pricked up.

How did you know that?

You seemed to *really* **hate that game when I suggested it.**

'I looked and looked but . . . he was gone,' she said sadly.
'Come with me,' I whispered. I led her over to the bone room entrance. 'Look closely.'

She had a good look around the room, but didn't see anything. 'I give up,' she finally said.

'**I win!**' Mr Fox shouted, emerging from his hiding place. He was very skinny and could barely walk. I'd been right—the mysterious eyes I'd seen earlier *had* belonged to him.

Mrs Fox covered him in kisses.

'I thought you'd never find me and that I'd starve to death' Mr Fox croaked. 'Is there still cake?'

'How about a serving of **lamb** before dessert?'
Mrs Fox said.
Both the foxes spun to face me. I turned and **fled**.

I found Billy, Shaama and the chooks waiting
for me down by a stream.

Billy had submerged himself in the **freezing water**. He refused to move until the scrunchies had been taken from his fringe. This meant it took twice as long to get home because he kept walking into things. He said he preferred it that way.

The sun was setting as we arrived at the entrance to the petting-zoo farm.

WELCOME

'I still can't believe you guys came to my rescue,'
I said to Billy and Shaama.

We lined up, like we were trying to buy tickets.
The old lady who works there shook her head
and made a tutting sound.
'Well, well, well, if it isn't the runaways.'
'We'd like to see the lamb, please,' I bleated.
'I hear he is adorably cute!'

We were let back in and the hens flew off, anxious to see their sisters again. Billy, Shaama and I walked over to our tree and sat down in an exhausted heap.

'Soak it up, guys,' I said, closing my eyes. 'We've **tamed** a bull and **beaten** a fox. Now it's time for this herd to have a well-earned break!'

But just as I began to relax, a shadow fell over us.

I looked up and saw **Ringo** and **Plus-sized Puss**.

'Finally, they show up,' Plus-Sized Puss purred.

You've been summoned. Come on.

'Summoned? Who's summoned us?' Shaama asked, backing away slowly.

'The pig,' Plus-sized Puss said. 'He's in the barn and he's not happy.'

'So what does he want with us?' Billy asked.

'Maybe he wants some comfy pillows to sit on,' Ringo said. 'Get moving!'

We weren't given any choice. Ringo bared his teeth and Plus-sized Puss flashed her claws.

The three of us were pushed into the barn. The fire was roaring hot and sitting beside it was **Kevin Bacon**.

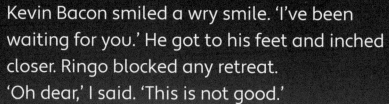

Kevin Bacon smiled a wry smile. 'I've been waiting for you.' He got to his feet and inched closer. Ringo blocked any retreat.

'Oh dear,' I said. 'This is not good.'

TO BE CONTINUED . . .

Will our fluffy friends be able to get out
of this one?

What does Kevin Bacon
want with **The Nerd Herd?**

Is that the last we've seen
of **Mr and Mrs Fox?**

Will **Janine's** feathers
ever grow back?

Find out in:
The Nerd Herd 4: Pig Out!